EGMONT

We bring stories to life

This edition published in Great Britain 2010 by Dean,
an imprint of Egmont UK Limited
239 Kensington High Street, London W8 6SA
All Rights Reserved

ISBN 978 0 6035 6521 2
3 5 7 9 10 8 6 4
Printed in Malaysia

Thomas, Emily and the Special Coaches

It was a fine summer on the Island of Sodor.

Gordon the big, blue engine had set a new record for pulling the Express. All the engines were very excited for him.

"I have a special surprise for you, Gordon," said The Fat Controller, one morning.

Proud Gordon blew his whistle as loudly as he could, "Peep! Peep!"

The Fat Controller had given Emily an important job. She had to pick up two very special coaches.

They had been newly painted to celebrate Gordon's record.

The Fat Controller was going to surprise Gordon with them.

Emily steamed along eagerly. "I must be on time, I must be on time," she puffed.

When Emily stopped to take on water, Diesel pulled up alongside her. "You look very pleased with yourself," he oiled.

Emily told him all about Gordon's record and collecting the coaches.

"Gordon's not the only one who's special," huffed Diesel.

"Well, there's nothing special about smelly old diesels," pouted Emily. "I haven't time to listen to you. I have to collect more coal."

And she steamed away, leaving Diesel looking cross.

Later, Emily arrived at the Yards.

But Gordon's special coaches
weren't there!

"Diesel has already collected them,"
puffed Thomas. "He said it was
his job."

"But that was my job," huffed Emily.
"I'll have to find them. I must not
be late for Gordon's presentation."

Emily raced quickly across the Island. "I must be on time, I must be on time," she puffed.

She was looking for Diesel and the special coaches.

Suddenly, Emily saw Diesel waiting at a signal.

He was coupled up to Gordon's special passenger coaches!

"Why have you taken Gordon's coaches?" Emily snapped, sharply.

"Because ..." Diesel began.

"I haven't got time to listen to you," huffed Emily. "Give me those coaches!"

"Not if you won't listen," grunted
Diesel. And he sped away, as fast
as his wheels would carry him.

Emily chased after Diesel.
"Come back!" she whistled.

It was getting later and later.

Emily was worried that the special
coaches would not be ready for
Gordon's presentation.

As usual, Diesel was being devious.
He knew all the tricks. And many
different tracks.

Poor Emily couldn't catch up
with him. Diesel made her look
silly!

"Please come back, Diesel!"
Emily whistled, sadly.

Emily steamed unhappily into
Maithwaite Station.

The Fat Controller was there,
waiting for Emily on the platform.
"Where are Gordon's special
coaches?" he asked her.

"Diesel took them, Sir," replied
Emily, quietly.

"We must find him at once!"
boomed The Fat Controller.
And he climbed into Emily's cab.

Diesel had hidden the coaches in a siding. But he wasn't feeling well and he had started to slow down.

Up ahead, Diesel saw Emily with The Fat Controller.

"Now I'm in trouble!" he groaned.

"Diesel," said The Fat Controller, sternly. "Where are Gordon's special coaches?"

"They're hidden in a siding, Sir," said Diesel, quietly.

"Take Emily there at once!" ordered The Fat Controller.

"Yes, Sir," replied Diesel.

Diesel took Emily to collect
the trucks from the siding.

Emily could see black smoke
coming from Diesel's engine.
"What's wrong with your engine?"
she asked.

"It's worn out from rushing around," said Diesel.

"Then you shouldn't have taken the coaches," huffed Emily.

"And you should have listened to me," Diesel replied, crossly.

Emily was puzzled. "Why should I listen to a smelly old Diesel?" she said.

"Because Gordon's not the only one who's set a record," said Diesel, quietly. "I've set one too."

Emily was surprised. "Have you?" she wheeshed. And this time she listened to Diesel.

"I've shunted more trucks in one day than any other diesel," Diesel said.

And he spluttered sadly away.

Emily began to feel sorry for Diesel.

"Diesel is just as special as Gordon," she said.

She wanted Diesel to feel special too, and thought of a clever idea.

Emily raced to Knapford Station with Gordon's special coaches rattling behind her.

She told The Fat Controller all about Diesel's record, and about her idea to make Diesel feel special.

The Fat Controller listened to Emily. "That's a very good idea, Emily," he said. "Tell Diesel to come here for the presentation this afternoon."

Later, at Knapford Station, The Fat Controller presented Gordon with his special coaches.

"Don't they look splendid!"
puffed Gordon, proudly.

Just then, Emily steamed into the
station. "And this new diesel motor
is for you, Diesel," she chuffed.

Diesel was very surprised.

"I'm sorry I didn't listen," said Emily.
"Now I know that diesels and
steamies are both special!"

Everyone cheered and whistled for
Gordon and Diesel! Peep, peep!